Disney's
Winnie the Pooh
Just Say "Thank You"

If someone

Gives you a present

Or does something nice,

Have the magic words ready.

Say them once

Or even twice!

C hristopher Robin hurried through the Hundred-Acre Wood carrying a present for his best friend, Pooh.

"I painted this just for you, Pooh," he said.

"It's perfect!" Pooh announced.

"Ahem . . . ," said Christopher Robin as they walked inside.
"What do you say, Pooh?"

"Oh, bother," Pooh scratched his head. "Perhaps I shall say,
'How about some honey while looking at my new painting?'"

"Silly ol' bear!" cried Christopher Robin. "Don't you know what to say when somebody does something nice for you? Don't you know the magic words?"

"You mean," pondered Pooh, "there are magic words?"

"In a way," said Christopher Robin, "because when you say them, it makes that person feel happy and appreciated."

"Oh," said Pooh. "Do you think I can try?"

"Why, of course, Pooh," Christopher Robin replied.
"Perhaps you should stand back," Pooh said.
Then he waved his paws in the air, trying to weave a magic spell.
"Abracadabra, fiddle-dee-doo, tiggledy-wiggledy!" cried Pooh.

Pooh spun around so fast he got dizzy—and landed headfirst
with a KERPLUNK right into a big pot of honey.

"Maybe you should think about it some more," said Christopher Robin, trying to get Pooh out of the honey pot.

Pooh licked his lips. "I'll do that, Christopher Robin," he promised.

Pooh decided he should ask some of his friends if they knew the magic words. First he found Eeyore resting in the sun.

"Magic?" said Eeyore. "Never did it myself. But I can try. Hum-drum, dum-dee-dum."

Pooh waited patiently, but nothing happened.
"I guess those weren't the magic words either," he said.
"Better luck next time," Eeyore said and went back to
his thistle patch.

Next, Pooh followed his nose to Rabbit's house.
Rabbit was pulling warm honey buns out of the oven.
"Perhaps I could try just one small one?" asked Pooh.

"Well . . . all right," sniffed Rabbit.
And with that, Pooh eagerly ate one of the honey buns.
But Pooh couldn't stop at just one. He ate another honey
bun . . . and another . . . and another, until he had eaten them all!

Pooh rubbed his tummy. "Are there any more?" he asked shyly.
"No," sighed Rabbit. "You've eaten them all! What do you have to say for yourself?"
"Oh!" cried Pooh. He'd forgotten about the magic words.

"Oh, bother!" mumbled Pooh, trying to remember the magic words.
Pooh concentrated very hard. "Hocus-pocus, yummy-tummy bear!"
he called, jumping high in the air.

"Stop!" cried Rabbit.

Pooh landed with a loud CRASH right in the middle of
Rabbit's mixing bowls, spilling the ingredients everywhere.
The kitchen was a sticky mess!

"Pooh Bear! What are you doing!?" cried Rabbit.

"Sorry, Rabbit," Pooh apologized. "I guess those weren't the right words, either."

Pooh left Rabbit's house rather quickly. He soon ran into Tigger. "Why so glum, chum?" asked Tigger, bouncing alongside Pooh. "I can't figure out the right sort of magic words," sighed Pooh.

"Magic words? Magic words? Well, you've come to the right place, Buddy Boy! Let me have a go at it!"

"Hippity-hoppity, spring-a-ding-ding!" Tigger bounced as he began to sing.

With each word, Tigger sprang higher and higher.
Soon he bounced so high that Pooh lost sight of him.
"Whoooo was that?" Owl asked from his window.
"It's Pooh and Tigger!" called Pooh from down below.

"I was wondering if you might know about the magic words, Owl. Are they working?" asked Pooh hopefully.

"I don't believe so," Owl answered.

"Sorry, Ol Paleroo. I tried," said Tigger.

Pooh looked under every leaf and rock for the magic words.
"Whatcha doin'?" asked Roo, hopping up to him.
"I'm searching for some special magic words, but I can't seem
to find them," said Pooh sadly.

"Maybe Mama could help you find them," said Roo.
"Whenever I lose one of my mittens, she's real good at finding it!"
So off they went to ask Kanga's advice.

Kanga listened patiently as Pooh told her his problem. "Oh, Pooh, try harder to remember," she said when he was finished. "There are two very special magic words to say when someone paints you a picture, shares a treat, or helps you out."

"Oh, bother," said Pooh, scratching his head. He was so deep in thought that he didn't even notice that all his friends had followed him to Kanga's. "Maybe I should just give up. Thank you anyway, Kanga."

Just then, Pooh realized what he had said. "Thank you! Thank you very much!" cried Pooh, overjoyed. And as all of his friends gathered around him, he shouted, "That's it! Those are the magic words!"

"You were right, Christopher Robin!" Pooh said excitedly. "These magic words make everyone feel special, and I'll never forget them again! Thank you, thank you all!"

A LESSON A DAY
POOH'S WAY

When it comes

to magic words,

"thank you" are two

of the very best.